THE CUPCAKED CRUSADER

To Catch a Clownosaurus

by Lawrence David
illustrated by Barry Gott

Dutton Children's Books · New York

For Tedwin Frank David, my youngest brother,
who, when he was three, wanted candy and my
mom wouldn't get him any, so he ran out of the
house and up the road to a very busy street,
and he ended up at the house of our family
dentist instead of the candy store.

—*L.D.*

Text copyright © 2003 by Lawrence David
Illustrations copyright © 2003 by Barry Gott

LIBRARY OF CONGRESS CATALOGING-IN-PUBLICATION DATA
David, Lawrence.
To catch a Clownosaurus / by Lawrence David; illustrated by Barry Gott.
p. cm. — (Horace Splattly, the cupcaked crusader ; #4)
Summary: When Horace and his schoolmates spend a weekend at a camp
in the Laffy Woods, the Cupcaked Crusader must cope with Mr. Dienow,
the diabolical science teacher, as well as his sister's dangerous search for
Blootinite, and the forest monsters known as Clownosauruses.
ISBN 0-525-47154-5 — ISBN 0-14-250135-2 (pbk.)
[1. Heroes—Fiction. 2. Camps—Fiction. 3. Monsters—Fiction.
4. Brothers and sisters—Fiction. 5. Humorous stories.]
I. Gott, Barry, ill. II. Title.   PZ7.D28232To2003   [Fic]—dc21   2003043228

Published simultaneously by Dutton Children's Books and Puffin Books,
divisions of Penguin Young Readers Group
345 Hudson Street, New York, New York 10014
www.penguin.com

Designed by Tony Sahara
Printed in USA

First Edition

1   3   5   7   9   10   8   6   4   2

To Catch a Clownosaurus

Other Horace Splattly Books:

Horace Splattly: The Cupcaked Crusader

Horace Splattly, The Cupcaked Crusader:
When Second Graders Attack

Horace Splattly, The Cupcaked Crusader:
The Terror of the Pink Dodo Balloons

Contents

THE CUTEST BABY YOU EVER SAW

Horace stood in the Happy Camper Megamart and looked around. In every direction, all he saw were legs and large shopping carts. Big mom-and-dad thighs bumped into his head. Small, sharp, kid elbows poked him in the ears. And worst of all, shopping-cart wheels ran over his toes. It wasn't easy being ten years old and still shorter than most six-year-olds. Horace was only thirty inches tall, exactly the same size as the box of Soily Boy Laundry Soap his mom had just put in the shopping cart.

Horace tugged on his mother's skirt. "Why do I need to bring laundry soap on the school trip?"

he asked. "We're only going away for two days."

Mrs. Splattly leaned down to her son. "What if one of your teachers asks you to do laundry in the lake? Don't you want to be prepared?" She stood up and read the paper in her hand. "Next on our list is a *canteen!*" she cheered. "I like the one in the shape of a kitty. Which do you like, honey?"

Horace stood on his tiptoes, but couldn't see the canteens on the shelves. Too many parents and kids were in the way. It seemed like tons of kids from Blootinville Elementary were shopping with their parents for next weekend's Teacher Bunk-Along at Camp Blite.

Horace tried to get closer to the shelves. One lady's big pocketbook swung right at his head like a wrecking ball about to smash down an old building.

"Whoa!" Horace cried, ducking in time. "I can't see anything."

"Well, I can take care of that," Mrs. Splattly said. She picked Horace up and placed him in the baby seat of the shopping cart. "Now you'll be able to see!"

Horace covered his face with his hands and peeked through his fingers. Sure, he could see all the stuff on the shelves, but now all the kids were staring at him sitting in the cart like a two-year-old. "Mom, get me out of here! I'm too old to sit in this!"

Cyrus Splinter pointed at Horace. Cyrus was the tallest kid in Blootinville Elementary by a foot and a half, and the meanest by eight and a half Blootometers. "Awww, isn't Horace the cutest baby you ever saw?" he shouted.

Sara Willow turned around and looked at Horace.

Horace's face turned red. He thought Sara was the prettiest thing he'd ever seen in his life. Every day she did her hair in a special, new way. Today her hairdo was shaped like a tent. Horace thought she looked prettier than a bowl of butterscotch pudding with whipped cream on top.

And now Sara was seeing him sitting in a shopping cart!

Sara whispered loudly in her mother's ear, "That boy's the same age as me and he's really little! He never ever grows an inch."

Horace took his mother's arm. "Please, Mom, put me back on the floor!"

Mrs. Splattly scrunched up her mouth. "Nonsense. Now tell me which canteen you like; otherwise I'll choose."

Horace reached into the shopping cart and grabbed his new baseball cap and sunglasses from the pile of stuff he'd be taking to camp next week. He put the hat and glasses on to hide his face. At least now no one would recognize him. He took a plain green canteen from the shelf. It had a whistle and magnifying glass attached to the strap. "This one's good," he said. He dropped it in the cart.

"I hope your father and Melody can find her a Lily Deaver combination bathing suit and tablecloth. Mrs. Honey told me those are very popular," Mrs. Splattly said. She looked at her list. "What else do you need?"

Horace peered into the cart. It had the laundry soap, a sleeping bag, underwear, sandals, hiking boots, sunscreen lotion, Small-Bug Stay-Away Spray, Large-Bug Stay-Away Spray, and a gallon jug of Toe Fungus Cream. "I think this is more than I need for such a short trip," he told his mom.

Mrs. Splattly tapped her list. "I know what we forgot!" she shouted. "Toilet paper!" She spun the cart around so fast, Horace's head jerked back.

"What do I need toilet paper for?" Horace asked. "Won't the camp have toilet paper?"

Mrs. Splattly rolled the cart down the toilet-paper aisle. "Ever since you were a baby, you've had a very tender tushy. I'd hate to think about you going away for even one day without your favorite brand of toilet paper." She grabbed a super-colossal pack of Sweet Cheeks Toilet Tissue off the shelf and put it in the cart. The toilet paper was white with pictures of green frogs on it.

"I don't need special toilet paper," Horace said, kicking his legs. "Don't treat me like such a baby."

Mrs. Splattly frowned. "This is your sister's and your first Teacher Bunk-Along, and I want you to be prepared for whatever happens. One day you'll thank me for buying you such fancy toilet paper."

Horace pulled the cap farther down over his face.

Cra-boom! A large crash was heard from the other side of the store.

"What could that be?" Mrs. Splattly asked.

The store's loudspeaker came on. "Red alert! Red alert! Exploding Strap Emergency in the swimsuit department! People in grave danger!"

Mrs. Splattly turned to Horace. "You stay right here. I'm going to check on your dad and sister." She ran down the aisle.

Horace wasn't sure what an Exploding Strap

Emergency was, but he was certain that the Cupcaked Crusader was the guy to help. Now all he had to do was figure out how to get his superpowers to work.

He reached into his pants pocket and felt a pile of crumbs from the cupcake his sister had made him eat yesterday.

Could a few crumbs give him enough super-powers to save people from an Exploding Strap Emergency?

These crumbs might.

• • •

The baker of the very special crumbs was Melody Splattly, Horace's younger sister.

Melody was a genius mad scientist and homemaker. She was already taller than her older brother, so she could make Horace do whatever she wanted or she'd beat him up. Once she invented a sink that could be rolled every-where, and she made her brother wash piles of her Lily Deaver scout uniforms in his bedroom. Another time she invented a frying pan that could tell your fortune, and she made her brother make hundreds of pancakes to test it. Horace used it all afternoon, but he always got the same fortune. It said, *Your sister will boss you around today.*

But of all Melody's inventions, the most amazing were her cupcakes. Melody baked special cupcakes that gave her brother superpowers for a little while. One cupcake gave him the power to fly so he could spy on a girl Melody didn't like. Horace thought he'd be able to show off his powers, but Melody said that wasn't allowed. She made him wear a special purple taffeta Cupcaked Crusader costume. She said that Horace always had to be in disguise when he had powers so no one would know who the Cupcaked Crusader was. Melody thought that if her parents found out, they'd take away her lavender Lily Deaver Spill & Brew Science Laboratory and her lavender Lily Deaver Cook & Bake Oven so she couldn't bake any more cupcakes.

Horace didn't always like doing the things

his sister wanted, but he did like having powers. That's why he agreed to wear the Cupcaked Crusader costume and keep his identity a secret.

Well, *almost* a secret. He had told his best friends, Auggie and Xax Blootin, about it and made them promise not to tell anyone. Especially not his sister. If she found out that they knew, she might get mad and make Horace eat a cupcake that gave him some power that turned his hands into mops or hair dryers or something dumb like that.

Just yesterday, Melody made Horace eat a cupcake that turned his fingers into knitting needles. Then she made her brother knit one hundred balls of lavender yarn into a blanket, sweater, socks, and skirt for her to bring on the Teacher Bunk-Along weekend. The only good thing about it was that because Horace had done such a good job knitting the clothes, Melody gave him two new cupcakes.

Of course, Melody wouldn't tell him what kind of powers the cupcakes had. "All I'll say is that they might come in handy when we're away at the Bunk-Along."

"I hope they don't turn my hands into erasers, so all I can do is clean blackboards," he told her.

Melody shook her head. "Heavens no, *little* brother," she said, giving Horace a pat on the head. "I promise they'll be much more exciting than that."

Horace packed the cupcakes in his knapsack under his Cupcaked Crusader costume to save for when he was at the Bunk-Along. Would they turn his hands into steam shovels? Would he grow rocket engines on his back so he could fly to the moon?

He didn't have a clue.

• • •

Horace may not have known what power those cupcakes would give him, but he did know he had to do something to stop the Exploding Strap Emergency. He didn't have his knapsack with his costume or cupcakes with him. He reached into his pocket and scooped out the pile of crumbs from the cupcake that had made his fingers into knitting needles. He licked them off his palm and swallowed.

He'd find out soon enough if these crumbs were enough to help. And he'd better be ready to become the Cupcaked Crusader.

Horace climbed out of the shopping cart. The aisle was empty. Everyone had rushed to the swimsuit section to see what was going on. He got in his thinking pose and put the forefinger of his left hand on his chin and the forefinger of his right hand in his ear and twisted it in a circle. He looked up and down the aisle at everything on the shelves. What could he use to make his Cupcaked Crusader costume?

And then he saw it. On the store shelf was a package of Lily Deaver Camper's Choice Lavender toilet paper.

Chapter 2

THE LAVENDER MUMMY

Moments later, Horace ran through the store with long knitting-needle fingers. He was wrapped from head to toe in the Lily Deaver toilet paper. The only part of him showing was his eyes. "Step back!" he called to the crowd by the swimsuit section. "The Cupcaked Crusader is here!"

The people gazed at Horace.

"The Cupcaked Crusader looks like a little Lily Deaver mummy," one girl said.

"He looks like a talking roll of butt paper," Cyrus Splinter said.

"What happened to your regular costume, Cupcaked Crusader?" Mrs. Splattly asked.

Horace stopped and thought of an answer. "Uh, it's at the cleaners. So what's the problem here?"

"Help us! Oh, help us, Cupcaked Crusader!" Mayor Blootin called.

In the center of the floor was a huge, tangled ball of hundreds of stretchy bathing suits. Arms and legs stuck out from the sides.

"What happened?" Horace asked the store manager.

"Well," the lady said, "about ten parents and kids were fighting over the swimsuits when the swimsuit rack fell over. Everyone got tangled in the different straps, drawstrings, arm and leg holes. Now they can't get out."

Horace raised his knitting-needle hands. "Everyone, please step back. This could be dangerous. I'd hate to snap a bathing suit and have it fly through the air and hit someone in the eye."

The crowd backed away.

"Help us!" a man called from inside the ball of swimsuits.

"Help me first, Cupcaked Crusader, if you know what's good for you!" Melody said.

"No, help me first," Auggie Blootin shouted.

"The elastics keep snapping in my face!" Dr. Splattly yelped.

Horace stuck his knitting-needle fingers into the pile, plucked out two bathing suit straps, and knit them together. Then he plucked out more and more straps and drawstrings and put those together. Sara Willow's head suddenly popped out of the ball. Her neck was stuck through the leg of a boy's bathing suit, and her tent hairdo had collapsed on top of her head. "Help!" she cried.

Horace snapped the elastic from around Sara's neck, and she climbed out of the ball. Within a few minutes, all the people had been freed, and the swimsuits had been knit into a quilt that looked like a map of the world.

Dr. Splattly shook Horace's hand. "Thank you for saving us, Cupcaked Crusader," he said. He pushed Melody toward her brother. "Tell the

Cupcaked Crusader how happy you are that he saved you."

"Don't be afraid of me," Horace joked with his sister.

Melody stared her brother in the eyes. "I am not afraid of you *ever*," she told him.

Just then, Penny Honey rolled by in her twenty-four-karat-gold chauffeur-driven shopping cart. The cart was filled with a backpack made out of emeralds and pearls, a handmade gold-and-diamond sleeping bag, and silver hiking boots decorated with rubies. "Hiya toodles," she cheered to Melody. "I'll see you tomorrow at the Bunk-Along! I'm going to buy all the most rare and expensive jewels in town and put them on my camping stuff!" The shopping-cart limousine rolled down an aisle and out of sight.

Melody stomped a foot. "That girl thinks she can have all the fancy stuff," she said to her parents. "It's not fair!"

Dr. Splattly shrugged. "Well, Penny and her family do have a lot of money," he said.

"Hmmmm," Melody thought aloud. "Well, I know of *one* rare gem no one has. It's called Blootinite, and I'm going to find it."

Horace spoke in his Cupcaked Crusader voice. "Little girl, no one's even sure Blootinite really exists, so how do you think you'll find it?"

Melody raised her nose in the air. "Ever since I was two years old and was able to read, I've been doing research at the library. And this weekend, I'm going to find Blootinite, then show it off and not let Penny Honey have *any*." She looked at her mom and dad. "Excuse me, but I have to go shopping for some tools, then we need to head home so I can finish some of my experiments." She turned her back and marched across the store.

Mrs. Splattly smiled at the Cupcaked Crusader. "I'm sorry if my daughter was a little rude, but she really doesn't like that girl." She took a camera from her pocketbook. "Would you mind if I took a picture of you with the mayor for the *Blootinville Banner*?" she asked.

"Oh, I'd like that!" Mayor Blootin said, putting his arm around Horace. "Take it with me and the twins."

Horace looked at Auggie and Xax, then down at his knitting-needle fingers. They had already begun to shrink. And his toilet paper costume was starting to tear. "Uh . . . uh . . ." Horace didn't know what to say.

Auggie stepped forward. "I don't think the Cupcaked Crusader likes his picture taken if he's not in his real costume," he said.

"Yeah, that's true," Xax agreed, stepping in front of Horace to block everyone from seeing his friend's knitting-needle fingers shrink. "It's probably bad luck."

Horace hid his hands behind his back. "Uh, yes, that's right. It's bad luck," he said. He wriggled out from under Mayor Blootin's arm, dashed across the store, and hid behind a garbage can. His knitting-needle fingers turned completely back to boy fingers. Horace tore the toilet paper from his body, stuffed it in the trash, and ran to the shopping cart where his mother had left him. As he tried to climb back in the cart, it tipped over, spilling all the camp stuff on top of him and pinning him to the ground.

"Help! Help!" Horace called. He stared up at the ceiling and heard people running toward him. The faces of his mom, dad, and sister looked down at him.

"Are you okay, honey?" Mrs. Splattly said. "Don't you know you're too little to get out alone?"

"Oh, Horace, please be careful," Dr. Splattly pleaded.

Melody knelt and whispered in her brother's ear. "Too bad the Cupcaked Crusader isn't here to save *you*," she said with a grin.

INTO THE WOODS

The bus to Camp Blite bounced along the dirt road through Laffy Woods. The busload of five- to ten-year-olds from Blootinville Elementary School had been on the road for over two hours. The fifty kids looked out the windows at the craggy boulders, huge trees, and animals that ran through the forest.

"Hey, I just saw an emu!" Cyrus Splinter screamed.

Mr. Dienow drove the bus. He was the school science teacher. "I *ate* four emus for dinner last night. They taste even better than children."

"Eeee-yuck! That's so disgusting," Myrna Breckstein said.

"Look at that!" Sara Willow shouted. "I saw a walrus climbing a tree!"

"Did you know that I had walrus pancakes for breakfast this morning?" Mr. Dienow asked.

"Eeee-yuck! That's so revolting," Myrna Breckstein said.

Horace, Xax, and Auggie looked out the windows.

"I hate Dienow," Horace said to the Blootin twins. "I can't believe he's going on the Teacher Bunk-Along weekend. He's the meanest teacher in the school. He always picks on me. I bet no kid in the whole school wants to bunk with him."

Screech! The bus came to a sudden stop.

Mr. Dienow stood up and walked over to Horace. "Did I hear you say you think that no kid in the whole school wants to bunk with me?" he asked.

Horace gulped. "Uh, n-no, sir," he answered.

"I—I said that only the l-luckiest kids in school would get to bunk with you."

Mr. Dienow smiled. "How sweet of you, my puny student," the teacher said, leaning close to Horace's face. "Maybe you'll be one of the lucky kids who gets to bunk with me." He turned around, took his seat, and began driving again.

Horace dropped his head into his hands. "Oh no," he said.

Auggie gave his friend a pat on the back. "Don't worry," he said. "Dienow was only teasing. Principal Nosair told me that he was going to be the teacher in the fourth-grade boys' bunk. Dienow's the teacher in the bunk with the kindergarten boys."

Horace swiped his hand across his head. "Phew," he said. "I couldn't ever last a whole weekend with Dienow. Thirty minutes in his classroom is bad enough."

Xax Blootin stared out the bus window. "Eight thousand seven hundred eighty-two, eight thousand seven hundred eighty-three," he said. "Eight thousand seven hundred eighty-four."

Auggie covered his twin's mouth with a hand. "Stop it! We know there are a lot of trees in the woods. It's obvious."

"But don't you want to know how many?" Xax asked.

Auggie rolled his eyes. "Why should I care how many trees there are?" he asked.

"Because it's fun," Xax said.

Horace pressed his nose against the window. "Remember last year when the Horndale family disappeared in Laffy Woods?" he asked.

Auggie took a sip from his celernip juice box. "I heard that they were found dressed in clown suits. And they never laughed again."

"That happens whenever anyone goes camping in Laffy Woods," Xax said. "But because the people who disappeared can't—or won't—say anything about what happened, no one believes anything's really wrong."

Horace took a look at his science teacher.

"I bet Dienow once went in the woods and got lost. That's probably why he never laughs except when something mean happens." Horace unzipped his backpack and took out the *Splattly & Blootin Big Notebook of Worldwide Conspiracies*. He opened it across his lap. "Here's our page called 'The People Who Got Lost in Laffy Woods Who Never Laugh Anymore,'" Horace said. He looked to his friends. "We should explore the woods and solve this mystery."

Xax shook his long blond bangs over his eyes. "But what if we get lost and never laugh again?"

Horace slipped the book into his backpack. "That won't happen to us," he whispered. "We're smarter than those other people, and I brought two of Melody's cupcakes with me, in case I need superpowers."

"That's great," Auggie said. "It will be fun to figure it out."

"I'd rather just count trees," Xax said.

A loud buzzing sound filled the air. An orange light flashed. "It works!" Melody yelled. "That signal means my radar detector's found Blootinite nearby!" She leaned over the back of her seat and shoved a weird box with a radar dish in the three boys' faces. "In your ancestor Serena Blootin's diary, she wrote that she found Blootinite near Rumbly Mountain, then hid it someplace where no one could find it. She said that it was the most beautiful jewel ever."

Auggie sat forward in his seat. "She also

wrote that no one *should try* to find it," he said.

Xax sat forward in his seat. "And she wrote that if someone did search for it, bad things might happen," he said.

"How do you know your detector works if you've never seen Blootinite?" Horace asked.

"That was easy," Melody said, switching off the Blootinite Detector. "Since I know what gems *do* exist, all I had to do was make a detector that would go off when it found a gem it didn't know."

Melody's best friend, Betsy Roach, popped her head over the back of the seat. "And I'm going to help you find it. Right, Melody?"

"That's right," Melody said. "We'll be the first Lily Deaver scouts *ever* to earn a Blootinite Badge of Honor." The girls squealed and turned back around in their seats.

The bus rounded a corner and hit a huge bump. All the kids bounced four feet out of their seats, then landed—*thwomp*—on their rear ends. Two chains bounced out from under Xax and Auggie's shirts. Hanging on each chain was a beautiful, shiny blue coin.

"What's that?" Horace asked.

"Just something our dad gave us before we left home this morning," Auggie said.

"He said they were our lucky camping coins that all Blootins take on their first camping trips," Xax said.

Both boys tucked the chains with the coins back under their shirts.

The bus finally came to a stop, and all the kids saw where they'd be spending the next two days of their lives.

On a patch of dirt by a lake stood one large twenty-foot-high dirt mound and ten smaller, cabin-size dirt mounds. "Welcome to Camp Blite," Mr. Dienow said with an evil laugh.

Chapter 4

CAMP BLITE

Mr. Dienow pulled the lever and swung open the bus door. "Everybody out!" he yelled. "OUT OUT OUT! There will be no dillydallying!"

The kids grabbed their gear from the overhead racks and hurried off the bus as fast as they could. They dropped their trunks onto the ground at their feet. The campground was soggy and had large puddles all over it. There wasn't any grass anywhere. Only dirt. *Wet* dirt. The kids' sneakers squooshed in the mud.

"This is blechy!" a boy yelled.

"Eeee-yuck! This place is so horrendous!" Myrna Breckstein said. She turned around and looked at Mr. Dienow. "Why is this place so horrendous?!"

Mr. Dienow scowled. "You kids are the only horrendous things I see," he answered. He swung the bus door shut and drove away behind the largest of the dirt mounds.

The kids looked at one another. None of their teachers were in sight. The place was completely silent except for the wind blowing through Laffy Woods.

Horace peered into the forest. "That wind sounds like it's laughing at us," he said. "And if you stare real hard, it looks like there's a bunch of eyes in the woods staring at us."

"Maybe it's the thing that makes people disappear every summer," Auggie said.

"I don't like it here!" five-year-old Petie Bloog said. He picked his nose, then lifted his shirt and stuck his finger in his belly button.

"Don't do that. It's gross!" Melody said.

"When I'm scared, I do this," Petie answered.

"I want my daddy!" six-year-old Henrietta Moorinsky cried.

Melody turned to Horace and Auggie. "Stop scaring the little kids," she said.

Sara Willow sat on her backpack. Today her hair was done in the shape of a large pinecone. "I wish the Cupcaked Crusader was here. He always knows what to do to make things right," she said in a dreamy voice. "I think he's the greatest."

Horace walked over to her. "Uh, maybe he'll come by later, but until he does, I can protect you."

Sara giggled. "You? You're almost the smallest kid here! I remember in the store your mom had to put you in the shopping cart so you wouldn't get stepped on."

Horace slunk back next to Auggie and Xax. "I think she likes the Cupcaked Crusader so much that she'll *never* like me now," he said.

Xax counted all the kids' footprints in the mud. "Do you think Dienow brought us to the wrong place on purpose?" he asked. "He hates kids, so do you think he would do that?"

Melody unfolded a large map. "According to

my research, this is the right place," she said. She pointed at the landscape. "That's Lake Honkaninny and that's Rumbly Mountain."

"But where are the teachers?" Cyrus asked.

"Where are we supposed to eat and sleep? This is all so eeee-yucky!" Myrna Breckstein said.

Melody tucked her map in her backpack. She turned in a circle, looking in every direction. All the kids' eyes were on her. "I don't know," she said quietly.

"Waaaaaaaaaah!" Petie Bloog and Henrietta Moorinsky cried, sounding like rusty lawn mowers.

"Stop sobbing or you'll make the ground muddier," Cyrus told them.

There was a loud whirring sound overhead. All the kids looked up. There in the sky was a pink-and-green-striped helicopter. And hanging down from it was a solid-gold log cabin. Penny Honey stood in the doorway waving. "Hiya too-dles, Melody! Isn't this all so very fan-ta-bulous!

I brought my own cabin along. I had it made special for this weekend. The chimney's made out of giant rubies!" Penny Honey's maid and butler waved from the windows. The helicopter set Penny's house by the edge of the lake, then flew away.

Melody gritted her teeth. "That girl's the worst. After I discover Blootinite, I'm going to buy a gold cabin ten stories high *and* a gold plane! Now, where are our teachers! Isn't anyone here?"

Creak.

The sound came from the large dirt mound.

A door opened in its side and out stepped a strange-looking man. He was dressed in a shiny white shirt, pants, and boots that had pockets all over them. In each pocket was a different-colored squirt bottle. The man wore a large, shiny, white squirt-bottle hat on the top of his head. "Hee-low, campers," the man said in a strange accent. "I'm Sir Stickle. I used to be a part of the royal family of the country Vinegary.

33

My family lost all our money, so we had to sell our kingdom. Now I run Camp Blite and work on making all sorts of glue." He pulled a purple squirt bottle from a pocket and stuck it in his mouth like he was a baby. "This is boysenberry glue. It's perfect for making Popsicle-stick birdhouses. It also tastes great."

He smiled. The purple glue covered the inside and outside of his mouth. "The hard part is getting it off your teeth, gums, and tongue." He reached inside his mouth, peeled the glue off his teeth, and stuck the mess in his pocket. "All my glues are special," Sir Stickle said. He pointed to a bottle on his stomach. "If you ever need to dance on top of a swimming elephant, this glue can help." He pointed to a bottle on his knee. "If you ever need to crawl across the ceiling while the house is blowing down, this glue can help."

"Uh, your glues are very interesting, Sir Stickle," Horace said politely, "but do you think you could tell us where our teachers are?"

Sir Stickle slapped a hand to his head. "I totally forgot! I'm supposed to introduce them!" He grabbed a bottle of bright gold glue from his pocket and sprayed it in the air, spelling out the letters W-E-L-C-O-M-E. After the sparkly glue hung in the air for a second, it all landed with a splat on Myrna Breckstein's head. Dirty leaves fell from trees and stuck to her hair.

"Eeee-yuck!" she cried.

Sir Stickle didn't seem to notice. He waved a hand in the air and shouted, "Announcing Principal Nosair and the teachers from Blootinville Elementary!"

Principal Nosair, five male, and five female teachers stepped out of the mud mound's door. Even though they were at a camp in the woods, they were wearing their suits and dresses just like they wore in the classroom. Ms. Wobbley-knees, the math teacher, was even carrying a miniature chalkboard and erasers with her. "Hello, campers!" the teachers shouted happily. "Welcome to the Teacher Bunk-Along!"

Sara Willow frowned. "Thanks for the welcome, but where are we going to *bunk-along*?" she asked. "I don't see any cabins."

Sir Stickle laughed. "Don't you see those mud huts? Where I come from, that's what everyone lives in. I built them from straw and dirt."

Principal Nosair smiled. "And each teacher decorated the inside of their hut to look like a classroom. It'll be just like sleeping in Blootinville Elementary! Isn't that great?" He reached into his pocket and pulled out a mini-notebook. "Now it's time to tell you your bunk names. The Inchworms is for our five-year-old boys. When I call your name, step forward in front of my brother Mr. Dienow. Petie Bloog, Chuck Foog, Brian Sloog, Mitch Zoog, and . . ." Principal Nosair slipped and fell on his face in the mud. When he stood, he wiped a smudge of mud off his cheek, picked up the list, and read, "And the last of our five-year-old campers in Inchworms is Horace Splattly!"

Bloog, Foog, Sloog, and Zoog stepped forward in front of Mr. Dienow.

Mr. Dienow snarled at Horace. "Mr. Splattly, aren't you going to join me?" he asked.

Horace stepped forward. "But I'm not five. Or six." He walked over to Principal Nosair. "You know I'm really ten. Everyone here knows I am."

"You look like you're four," Cyrus said.

"But he's *really* ten," Auggie said.

Horace tugged on the principal's arm. "I know I'm short, but I *am* ten. I should be in the bunk with the other fourth-grade kids. Mr. Dienow knows that."

Principal Nosair looked at his brother. "But you told me Horace should be in your bunk, didn't you?"

Mr. Dienow nodded. "On the bus ride he said he wanted to be in my bunk. I didn't want to disappoint him." He winked at Horace and grinned an evil grin.

"But I'm ten!" Horace said. He stomped his

foot, and mud splattered across his face.

Principal Nosair shook his head. "Well, you did say you wanted to be in my brother's bunk, and the ten-year-old bunk is full. If you don't bunk with the Inchworms, there won't be a bed for you here. Don't worry, I'm sure you'll have a great time bunking with my brother. He's a very funny guy."

All the kids looked at one another. No one else thought Mr. Dienow was a very funny guy.

Mr. Dienow smiled at Horace. "Come along, Mr. Splattly. Let's go have a very, very fun time."

"Hey, don't worry, little kid. I promise not to pick on you too much," Bloog said.

Horace looked to Auggie and Xax. "Guess I'll see you later, if Dienow doesn't kill me first," he whispered. He picked up his camping gear and followed Dienow and his bunkmates across the yard to their mud hut.

Chapter 5

DIENOW'S HUT

The outside of the Inchworm hut may have been mud and straw, but inside was a different story. Dienow had decorated the hut to look exactly like his science classroom. Instead of desks, there were five cots with straps that went across them like belts, and each cot was attached to a whole bunch of wires.

Horace saw that the wires were attached to a large battery that stood in the corner of the room. "Uh, Mr. Dienow, why do the beds have belts on them and why are they attached to that battery?"

"Let me show you," Mr. Dienow said. He lifted Horace and dropped him onto one of the cots. He took the belt and fastened Horace to the cot, then went to the corner and grabbed a large switch. "This is an experiment I'm going to let you help me with. After thirty seconds, you'll feel like a completely different boy."

"Hey, get me off this!" Horace called. "I don't want to be a completely different boy!"

Foog, Sloog, and Zoog started crying. "No no no no!" they screamed. "Don't hurt us!"

Petie Bloog cried, then stuck his finger in his nose.

Dienow rolled his eyes. "Babies! You're all babies!" He walked over to Horace and unstrapped him from the bed. "I guess I'll just have to do it when you're all asleep in your beds," Dienow said into Horace's ear.

Foog, Sloog, and Zoog stopped crying and looked at Bloog.

Bloog took his finger out of his nose and stuck it in his belly button.

"Look at him," Foog said to Sloog.

"He's a booger belly baby!" Sloog said.

"Booger belly baby," Zoog called at Bloog.

Mr. Dienow laughed. "Yes, Petie Bloog is a booger belly baby, isn't he?"

Foog, Sloog, and Zoog stood in a circle around Bloog. "Booger Belly Baby! Booger Belly Baby! Booger Belly Baby!" the five-year-olds chanted.

Petie Bloog ran away from them and over to Horace. "I don't have any friends," he said.

Horace pulled Petie's hand out of his belly button. "Stop picking your nose and putting it in your belly button. Then the kids won't call you a Booger Belly Baby," he said. Horace couldn't believe he had to hang around with kindergartners.

Mr. Dienow clapped his hands. "Okay, babies. Unpack all your gear, then we'll have our first Teacher Bunk-Along class."

Horace picked up his backpack and set it on a cot. "What kind of class will that be?" he asked.

Mr. Dienow took a large pair of rusty nail clippers out of his pocket. "We'll do an experiment to see who has the strongest toenails! Won't that be fun?"

Foog, Sloog, and Zoog started crying again.

Petie Bloog started crying and stuck his finger in his nose again.

"Babies!" Dienow shouted. "You're all babies! Don't any of you want to do experiments with your toenails?!"

Horace slumped down on his cot. Between the little kids' crying and Dienow's crazy experiments, he was afraid this was going to feel like a *very* long weekend.

THE FIRST LAUGH

After about twenty minutes, Sloog, Foog, and Zoog stopped crying long enough to unpack their clothes.

Dienow told the boys that if they cried anymore, he'd get glue from Sir Stickle and glue all their eyes and mouths shut. He even told Petie Bloog that if he didn't stop picking his nose and putting it in his belly button, he'd get some special glue and fill Petie's nose and belly button with it.

That made Petie Bloog cry louder, and the other kids teased him more.

Horace stayed by his cot. He didn't want anything to do with the little kids. He couldn't wait until dinnertime so he could hang out with Auggie and Xax. He unpacked all his clothes onto the shelves except for his Cupcaked Crusader costume, which he kept hidden in the bottom of his knapsack.

After all, with Dienow as his bunk-along teacher, who knew what might happen? Would Dienow strap him to his cot and really do some scary electric experiment on him? Or would Dienow use his gigantic clippers to do weird things to his toenails?

Horace didn't know the answer, but he wanted to make sure his two cupcakes and costume were ready just in case he needed to become the Cupcaked Crusader in a hurry.

● ● ●

At six o'clock, all the kids and teachers lined up for a dinner of hot dogs, burgers, corn on the cob, and mashed celernips. Penny Honey ate at her own solid-gold picnic table. Her plate was gold, her cup was gold, and even her hot dog, corn, and celernips had been sprayed with a special gold sauce. Melody hissed with anger every time she looked at Penny Honey.

Horace shared a table with Auggie and Xax. He told them about his hut, and they told him about theirs.

"We're in the Cougar hut with Principal Nosair," Auggie said.

"He's really nice, just like at school," Xax said. "We watched movies on the wall of the hut, and he showed us his miniature pet goat named Flouncey."

"Wow, that sounds like a great Teacher Bunk-Along," Horace said. "Dienow just tries to do scary experiments and makes the little kids cry."

Petie Bloog set his plate and bottle of celernip soda by Horace. "I sit with you," he said. "The other kids say I'm icky."

Horace sighed. There was no escaping this kid. "Okay," he told Petie. "Come on and sit with us. Auggie and Xax, this is Petie Bloog; he's one of my bunkmates."

The sun began to set behind Rumbly
Mountain. The kids and teachers dug into their
meals. A soft wind blew, rustling the leaves on
the trees—and the leaves that were still stuck in
Myrna Breckstein's hair.

Hahahahaha . . . hahahahaha . . .

"That laughing is coming from the woods!"
Horace leaped out of his seat. "I bet it's a monster that catches people and stops them from
laughing anymore!"

"Sit down, Horace," Auggie hissed.

"Shut up about that," Xax said. "Everyone heard you."

Horace gazed around the campsite. All eyes were on him.

Mr. Dienow came over to Horace, patting him on the head. "I know you're not very smart, but that's just the noise the wind makes when it blows through the trees, little baby," he said. He pushed Horace back down in his seat. "That's why this forest is called Laffy Woods. If it scares you too much, we could tuck you in a crib with a blankie. Would you like that?"

All the kids and teachers laughed except for Auggie, Xax, and Horace.

Cyrus Splinter smiled at Horace. "Are you scared like a baby from the Inchworm bunk?" he asked. "Do you want to sit on my lap?"

Horace scowled at him. "No, I'm not scared," he said.

Sara Willow leaned over to the girl sitting next to her and said, "His mom makes him sit in the shopping cart when he's at the store."

Hahahahaha . . . hahahahaha . . . the woods laughed.

Horace kept his mouth shut. He'd prove to everyone that there was a monster in the woods. *And* that he wasn't too scared to find it.

• • •

Night had fallen. The camp was lit by a full moon. Gray clouds drifted through the sky, casting shadows across the lake. Kids talked to their teachers about school, made schoolbooks from tree bark, or sang songs with their teachers about how much fun it would be to live at school all the time. Melody, Betsy, and the other girls from their bunk huddled in a circle. Melody switched on her Blootinite Detector, and the machine's light blinked off and on really fast. "We're going to find the jewels really soon," Melody told the girls. "I just know we will!"

Horace, Auggie, and Xax walked along the lake. Petie Bloog chased after them. "Don't run with fast feet," he said. "I don' wanna get disappeared."

"Then walk faster," Horace called. He turned to Auggie and Xax. "Sorry that kid's following us," he told them.

The three boys sat down in the sand and dipped their toes in the water.

Hahahahaha . . . hahahahaha . . .

A chill ran down Horace's spine. "I think Dienow's wrong. The wind in the trees doesn't sound like that at home. Something's in there watching us," he said.

Auggie splashed his feet in the water. "Well, don't tell everyone more about it until we have proof," he said. "Otherwise you'll make us all look stupid."

Horace stared hard into the woods. "I was warning everyone so no one got hurt," he explained. "Don't you think it's important to do that?"

"Let's find the monster first, then warn everyone second," Auggie said.

"I don't want to find anything," Xax said. "I kind of think Horace is right. Something really is watching us."

Horace leaned forward. "Do you see it, too?" he asked Xax. "Look over there by the dock. There are a bunch of eyes looking at us."

"A bunch of eyes?" Auggie asked. "All I see is the dark night."

"Look more carefully," Horace said.

"Yeah," Xax said.

The three boys stared into the woods.

Hahahahaha . . . hahahahaha . . .

"Hey!" Petie Bloog yelled from behind them.

"Shhhh, Petie," Horace called. "Sit down with us and keep quiet. We're doing some investigating."

Hahahahaha . . . hahahahaha . . .

"Hey, leave me 'lone!" Petie Bloog yelled.

"We're not even near you," Auggie said.

"Is someone else there?" Horace asked Petie. Horace stood and looked along the shore for his bunkmate. A cloud passed in front of the moon, and everything turned pitch-black. The only thing the boys could see were twelve shiny orange eyes glowing from the woods at the edge of the lake.

"Do you see them now?" Horace asked Auggie.

"Uh, yeah, I see 'em," Auggie said, grabbing Horace's arm.

"What do we do?" Xax said, grabbing Horace's other arm.

"What are you doing?" Petie asked someone. Or some*thing*.

Horace couldn't see Petie or whom he was talking to. "Petie, where are you? We're right here. Keep walking," he called.

Hahahahaha . . . hahahahaha . . .

"Petie? Are you there?" Horace called. "Petie!"

The cloud cleared the moon. A beautiful blue light lit up the lake.

Hahahahaha . . . hahahahaha . . .

Horace, Auggie, and Xax stared down the shore. There in the sand stood Petie. He was now dressed in a white baggy costume with colored spots, a pointy hat, and large floppy shoes. His face was painted white, and a red lightbulb blinked on his nose.

"Wh-what happened?" Horace, Auggie, and Xax asked all at once.

"Clownosaurus," Petie said. "They told me they were Clownosauruses."

Chapter 7

SECRETS & LIES

Horace and the Blootin twins sat Petie in the sand.

"What did the Clownosauruses say?" Horace asked.

"What did they want?" Auggie asked.

"How many are there?" Xax asked, looking all around. "Are there only three?"

Petie shook his head and stuck his finger in his nose. "I'm scared," he said. "The biggie told me we go or they get us and we can't ever laugh anymore."

Horace's eyes opened wide. "I can't believe it! We've found them!"

Auggie gave Horace a look. "We didn't *find*

them. They found *us*! And they want us to leave."

Xax looked at Petie in the clown suit and began counting all the spots on it. "I—I don't want to be turned into a clown, Horace."

Horace stomped a foot in the sand. "Don't be silly. This is excellent," he exclaimed. "After we catch the Clownosaurus and show it to everyone, we'll be great discoverers that everyone writes about in books! Don't you want to be in the history books so all the kids have to read about us in school? Then I bet they'll even let me move into the fourth graders' hut and kick Cyrus into the Inchworms with Dienow!"

Auggie picked up a rock and tossed it in the lake. "I think we should just tell a teacher," he said. "That's probably the right thing to do."

"Exactly," Xax said.

"Tell teacher," Petie said.

"No way," Horace said. "Just think about how amazing it would be to find a real Clownosaurus. Don't you want to see one?"

Sir Stickle walked up behind them and leaned over the boys' heads. He was sucking on a bottle of pink glue. "What's going on, campers?" He smiled. "Aye there, Bloog. Why the clown duds? Those your pj's?"

Horace put a finger to his lips. Auggie, Xax, and Petie all looked from him to Sir Stickle. None of them said a word.

"Don't I get an answer?" Sir Stickle asked. His face got serious. He knelt by Petie. "Bloog, did these boys do this to you? Is that why you're not squawking?"

Petie shuffled his floppy clown feet. His red nose blinked, lighting up his face. "Uh, n-no, they didn't," he said.

"Then how'd you get the clown-wear?" Sir Stickle asked.

"I dunno," Petie said.

Sir Stickle looked at the four boys carefully. "Well, I hope everything's swell. Now let's get to bed. Tomorrow's a big day. All the teachers will be taking their bunks on survival hikes into the woods."

"I—I don't want to go in the woods," Petie said. "That's where the Clowno—"

Horace stepped forward. "Petie just wants to wear his clown suit, but doesn't think he could wear it when he's hiking," he interrupted.

Sir Stickle laughed. "That's true, Bloog. You probably shouldn't go hiking in a clown suit. But you can wear it to bed tonight if Mr. Dienow says it's okay." He walked off down the beach. "Come along. Time to hit the hay."

The four boys strolled the beach, following Sir Stickle.

Horace beamed. "Let's keep this our secret so we can be the first ones to find a Clownosaurus," he said. "Maybe we'll see one tomorrow in the woods."

Petie looked frightened.

Xax looked terrified.

Auggie looked concerned. "I'm not sure about this, Horace. What if the Clownosauruses come back?"

Horace smiled at the thought of catching a Clownosaurus. Would his parents let him keep one for a pet?

"Horace, don't you think we should warn everyone?" Auggie asked.

Horace shook his head. "Absolutely not. Remember you said we shouldn't say anything until we get proof? We don't really have proof now, do we? We haven't seen one yet, have we?"

"Uh, I guess not," Auggie agreed.

Horace kept walking. "Anyway, I have a feeling a certain superhero will watch over us so no one gets hurt."

THE DISAPPEARING TEACHERS

Horace lay in bed, his eyes shut. Sunlight shined through his eyelids.

"Where'd he go?" Floog asked.

"'S not in his bed," Zoog said.

"'S not outside," Sloog said.

"'S not in dining place," Petie Bloog said.

Horace sat up and rubbed his eyes. The first thing he saw was Petie Bloog in the clown suit standing by Dienow's bed. Petie stuck a finger in his blinking clown nose, then stuck it in his clown-suit belly button.

"Now the Booger Belly Button Baby's a Booger Belly Button Bozo," Floog said.

The three boys laughed at Petie.

"Stop teasing him," Horace said, rolling out of bed. "Is Dienow gone? Are we getting a new teacher in our bunk?" He woke up afraid he'd find his body strapped to the cot and Dienow shocking him with electricity. It was great news to hear his evil science teacher had left the bunk for good.

"Not just Dienow," Floog said. "They're all gone."

"We found a word on his bed," Sloog said.

Horace put on his bathrobe. "What are you talking about?"

Zoog handed Horace a note. "Here's the word," he said. "We couldn't read it."

Horace read the note aloud, "It says, 'Don't.'" He turned the paper over, but there were no more words on it. He padded across the floor to the hut door and pushed it open.

The sun lit all of Blite Camp, sparkling on the

lake like a diamond and drying out the muddy ground.

Auggie and Xax appeared in the doorway of their hut. They were wearing matching pajamas that were decorated with pictures of famous movie stars eating celernips. Horace waved. "Have you guys seen Dienow?" he asked.

Auggie brushed his blond bangs over the top of his head. Xax shook his blond bangs over his eyes. "Not around here," Auggie said. "Have you seen Principal Nosair?"

"He's missing, too?" Horace asked.

"The only thing on his bed was this piece of paper with the word 'Again,'" Auggie said.

Penny Honey's maid leaned out her cabin door. "Children, could you please keep it down? Miss Honey is getting her beauty sleep."

Melody and Betsy appeared in the door of the Mangler hut. Both were wearing their Lily Deaver lavender feather pajamas. "Hey, kiddettes, have you seen Ms. Wobbleyknees?" Melody asked. "All she left behind was a note taped to her chalkboard. It says, 'Go.'"

"Dienow's also missing," Horace said.

Sara Willow leaned out her cabin window. "Miss Cuddles is also missing," she said.

Other kids began appearing in the doors of all the huts.

"Where's Mrs. Dot?" a girl asked.

"Where's Mr. Polka?" a boy asked.

From hut to hut, all the kids asked where their teachers were and said that all they found were notes with one word.

"Hey, look!" Melody yelled. "Read the words starting with the youngest boys' hut and going to the oldest girls' hut!"

All the kids' heads turned in a circle as they read the pieces of paper from hut to hut to hut.

The words spelled out the message, "Don't look for Blootinite. Go home or never laugh again."

• • •

Ten minutes later, the kids were dressed and in

the large hut that was the camp's dining hall. They tacked the pieces of paper up in order and reread the message.

"Where could they have gone?" Amanda Hightop asked.

"What happens if we don't go home?" Sid Blid asked.

"Why would anyone care if I'm looking for Blootinite?" Melody asked.

Cyrus climbed up on a table and cupped his hands around his mouth like a megaphone. "I think the teachers went back to Blootinville," he announced. "And we should, too. I don't care about Blootinite, so let's get out of here!" He took out his cell phone and dialed. All the kids watched him. Cyrus listened, frowned, and tossed his phone to the floor. "There's no signal. It doesn't work."

"How do we get home?" Myrna Breckstein asked. "We don't have a ride."

"We can't go home without the teachers," Horace said. "We have to help them."

"Help them do *what*?" Cyrus asked.

Melody held up her Blootinite Detector. Its orange light flashed over and over again. "I don't care whether they disappeared or not. All I know is that I'm close to discovering Blootinite and I'm not going anywhere without it."

Horace shook his head. "I wouldn't do that. This could be more dangerous than you think," he told his sister.

Melody put her hands on her hips. "How would you know?"

Horace took Petie and led him to the front of the crowd of kids. "Petie, tell everyone what happened last night with the Clownosauruses."

"What's a Clownosaurus?" Cyrus asked. "Did your little pea brain dream that up last night?"

"My brother's always dreaming dumb stuff," Melody said, looking Horace right in the eyes. "Once he even dreamed *he* was the Cupcaked Crusader!"

All the kids laughed except for Horace, Auggie, and Xax.

Horace waved his arms. "But it's real!" he shouted. "One of them got Petie last night and told him to tell us to go away. Auggie, Xax, and I were there. And because we didn't leave, they must have come and got the teachers!"

All the kids looked at Horace, Petie, Xax, and Auggie. Petie's nose blinked on and off.

Horace gave Petie a nudge with an elbow. "Go ahead. Tell them about the Clownosauruses," he said.

Petie's knees knocked together, his nose blinked faster, and he ran out of the dining hall without saying a word.

Cyrus slammed a foot to the table to get everyone's attention. "Listen, everyone, there's no such thing as a Clownosaurus," he said. "And since there are no teachers here and I'm the biggest kid, I'm in charge and everyone has to do what I say. My plan is that all the little kids will build a giant wagon and pull all the big kids back to Blootinville. Now let's get outside and start cutting down trees."

Melody stepped forward and climbed on top of another table. "I'm not building a wagon to pull anyone home! I came here to discover Blootinite and I'm going to do it!"

Horace walked over to her. "You can't go into the woods. The Clownosauruses will get you if you try to find Blootinite. Remember the message?" he said.

Melody turned up her nose. "I don't think there's any such thing as a Clownosaurus. I think you're probably making it up. I've never seen *anything* about a Clownosaurus in all the books I've read about Blootinite and Laffy Woods. There isn't even a Lily Deaver *badge* for a Clownosaurus, so I know it can't be real."

"They *are* real," Horace said. "They're the ones who put Petie in that clown suit."

Cyrus laughed. "Monsters came and put Petie in a clown suit? That's the stupidest thing I ever heard, pea brain."

All the kids laughed except for Horace, Xax, and Auggie. Even Sara Willow laughed.

Melody scowled at her brother. "I think Xax, Auggie, and Horace woke up early and made up the whole Clownosaurus story so they could try and scare us! I think they just don't want me to discover Blootinite before they do." Melody smiled at the other four girls in her hut. "Manglers, join me on a trip into the woods, and we'll find the most beautiful jewel ever and get richer than Penny Honey!" She stepped from the table to the chair to the floor and marched out of the room, followed by all the other girls from her hut.

"You can't do that!" Horace called after her.

Cyrus called out to the other kids, "Everyone, head outside. I want our wagon built by sundown tomorrow, or me and my goons will tie you all to trees, put peanut butter in your noses, and let the birds peck them." Michael Ma and Saul Shlock lifted Cyrus off the table and carried him out of the hut on their shoulders, followed by all the campers except for Auggie, Xax, and Horace.

Auggie folded his arms across his chest. "Well, Horace, you made us keep the Clownosauruses a secret and now the teachers are missing, Cyrus is taking over the camp, and your sister is going into the woods to find Blootinite."

"What should we do?" Xax asked.

Horace got into his thinking pose. He put the forefinger of his left hand on his chin and the forefinger of his right hand in his ear and twisted it in a circle. He thought long and hard, then longer and harder. "Guys, there's only one thing we can do," he finally announced. "The three of us will form a secret rescue team to guard the Manglers, save the teachers, and catch a Clownosaurus!"

LEADER OF THE PACK

Horace, Auggie, and Xax walked out of the hut.

About forty kids were slaving away on the field. Some were chopping trees. Some were sawing logs into planks. Some were hammering the planks and starting to build the wagon. The kids kept flopping onto the ground. Mud spattered their shoes, knees, elbows, faces, and necks.

Standing over them was Cyrus Splinter. He stood in the lifeguard chair by the lake. Sitting next to him was Sara Willow.

Cyrus waved a stick in the air. "Those are the

wrong kind of trees!" he barked, pointing his stick. "I want *birch* trees, not *pine* trees! Don't you want the wagon to look nice? You other kids are sawing the wood the wrong way. Go against the grain! If my girlfriend Sara gets one splinter when she sits in that wagon, I'll make you start all over again!"

Sara Willow punched Cyrus's arm. "I'm not your girlfriend! I'm only sitting up with you so I don't have to work!"

Cyrus grinned at her. "Awww, c'mon, Sara.

Once you get to know me, I *know* you'll want to be my girlfriend."

Horace gasped. "He can't make Sara his girl-friend! She doesn't even want to be his girlfriend!"

Cyrus pointed his stick at Myrna Breckstein. "Hey, little girlie with the curly hair, you're not hammering hard enough! If any of those nails fall out, I'll make you eat them for lunch!"

Myrna Breckstein raised her head. Mud covered half her face, and an acorn was stuck to her nose. "But I'm hungry. We haven't had breakfast yet," she said sadly. "Why does it have to be all so very eeee-yucky?"

Cyrus's face turned as red as a tomato in strawberry sauce with a cherry on top. "You'll get breakfast after you've earned breakfast!" he decreed. "For every hour of work, you'll get one slice of bread and one cup of water. If you work real hard, you'll also get a handful of raisins. Now shut up. I don't want to hear one word from any of you, or I'll have my boys shut you in jail like Petie Bloog. He wouldn't work and look what I did to him!" Cyrus pointed his stick at one of the huts.

Across the yard, one of the huts had thick wooden bars in the windows, and Michael Ma and Saul Shlock guarded the door. Ketchup and mustard were painted on their faces to make them look meaner than usual. Petie Bloog's sad face could be seen in the hut's window. His small hands gripped the bars.

Horace grabbed Auggie and Xax's arms and yanked them behind some bushes.

"Hey, what are you doing?" Xax said, rubbing his shoulder. "You almost discombobulated me."

"What's the deal?" Auggie asked, stepping out from behind the bushes.

Horace pulled him back. "Don't let Cyrus see you or he'll make us his slaves," he said. "There's no time to lose—we have to start saving everyone. You guys go to your cabin and start packing for our mission. I'm going to see what Melody is up to. We'll meet at my cabin in five minutes."

Auggie gave Horace a hard stare. "Who said we want to go into the woods and put ourselves in danger? Is this just because Cyrus is trying to make Sara his girlfriend?" he asked. "It seems a lot easier to do what Cyrus says than to do what you say."

"Yeah," Xax agreed. "You're just making us your slaves the same way Cyrus is doing to the other kids."

Horace sat on the ground. The twins were right. He was being just as bossy as Cyrus.

"Sorry," he said. "I just wanted to hurry and save everyone. If you want, one of you guys can be in charge."

Auggie and Xax looked at each other.

"Should it be you or me?" Auggie asked. "I think me."

Xax wrinkled his mouth. "I think *me*," he said.

Auggie took his lucky coin from around his neck. On one side was a picture of Serena Blootin. On the other side was a picture of a celernip along with the Blootinville town motto: *Don't sit on a celernip or you'll smash it.*

"What are you going to do with your lucky coin?" Horace asked.

Auggie slipped it off the chain. "I'll flip it to see if Xax or I get to be the leader," he said. "Call it," he told his brother.

"Heads," Xax said.

"Then it's tails for me." Auggie tossed the coin in the air, caught it, and slapped it to the back of his hand.

Heads.

"I'm the leader," Xax said.

Auggie frowned, strung the coin back around his neck, and tucked it under his shirt.

Horace looked at Xax. Xax had never made a plan before, and Horace wasn't sure what kind of leader he'd be. Horace had wished Auggie would win the coin toss. "Uh, so what's your plan going to be, Xax?"

Auggie spoke up. "Don't make it something we have to do thirty-one times just because that's your favorite number. And don't make it anything that has to do with counting either."

Xax crouched on his knees and made three Xs in the sand. He circled the first X. "One. We go see what's up with Melody." He drew an arrow to the next X. "Two. We go to our hut and pack for our foray into Laffy Woods." Xax made an arrow to the third X. "Three. We run over to the Inchworm hut, so Private Splattly can pack his gear. Are we clear, troops?"

Auggie laughed in his brother's face. "Why are you talking like that?"

Xax brushed his long bangs over his eyes. "Isn't that how army generals talk?" he asked with a grin.

"It sure is," Horace said. "You're kind of scary."

Xax got serious again. "Well, soldiers, that's how it's got to be." He brushed his palm across the dirt, erasing the plan. "Okay, team, it's time to start Operation Clownosaurus."

Chapter 10

OH WHERE, OH WHERE, HAVE OUR MANGLERS GONE?

Team Xax made its way around Camp Blite, hiding behind the huts so Cyrus wouldn't see them. Horace and Auggie crouched on the ground, and Xax stood on their backs to peek inside a screen window.

"Hurry up," Horace said. "You're not as light as you look."

The heel of one of Xax's boots slipped onto his brother's face.

"Hey!" Auggie called. "You stepped on my cheek."

"What do you see?" Horace asked.

Xax stood on the toes of his boots to get a better look. "Wow! The floors, walls, and ceiling are all chalkboards covered with tons of math problems. Even the beds have math problems written all over them."

Auggie raised a hand and hit his brother's leg. "We don't care how the cabin's decorated."

"Yeah," Horace said, wriggling under Xax's foot. "Just tell us what my sister's doing. That's what we came here to find out."

Xax stepped off the boys' backs. "Don't talk to me like that. I'm your leader. Show some respect."

Auggie and Horace stood up. A footprint from Xax's boot covered half of Auggie's face.

"Uh, General Xax, could you please tell us what you saw in the hut, sir?" Horace asked.

Xax paced back and forth before the boys. "I'm sorry to report that all the Manglers are gone, as are their backpacks, sleeping bags, and your sister's Blootinite Detector."

"We're too late," Horace exclaimed. "Nothing stops my sister when she gets some stupid idea in her head."

"How will we ever find them?" Auggie asked. "Laffy Woods is gigantic."

Horace got into his thinking pose and thought long and hard, then longer and harder. He knew exactly what they needed to do. "What we should do is—"

Xax lifted his head. "Private, I'm the officer in charge, and I'll decide what our next course of action will be."

Auggie took his brother by the shoulders. "This is serious, Xax. If we don't find Melody, the Clownosaurus could catch her."

Xax puffed out his chest like a rooster. "Am I in charge of this mission or not?"

Auggie glanced at Horace. "Uh . . . "

Xax looked to Horace. "Am I the officer in charge or are you, Private?" he asked.

Horace bit his lip to keep from laughing. He lifted a hand and saluted Xax. "Yes, sir. You're the officer in charge, sir. So what do we do next, General?"

Xax lifted his chin high and began marching. "Private Splattly, I believe it's time you ate one of your special cupcakes. We need to send you into the woods to locate Melody Splattly. I'd also like you to keep an eye out for any Clownosauruses and teachers. Then you'll report back to base camp, and we'll all head into Laffy Woods for our rescue mission. Is your assignment clear?"

Horace bit his lip again and saluted Xax. "Yes, sir, General Xax."

"Is that clear with you, Private Blootin?" Xax asked his twin.

Auggie rolled his eyes. "That's fine, General Xax. Now can we get moving? Melody has already been gone for over an hour."

Xax nodded slowly. "Good thinking, Private. Forward, march!" He marched a step, slipped, and fell facedown in the mud.

"Forward, flop." Auggie laughed.

• • •

Inside the Inchworm hut, Auggie examined the cupcakes Horace had brought with him. General Xax told Auggie that he could decide which cupcake Horace should eat because he had to go in the bathroom to wash mud off his face. But Xax did order that Horace shouldn't eat the cupcake until he was back in the room and in charge again.

Auggie and Horace sat on the cot. Auggie picked up one cupcake, then the other. "Do you know what these cupcakes do?" he asked Horace.

Horace shook his head. "I don't know. I think Melody made them so they'd give me powers to help her find Blootinite."

One cupcake was bright red and had a black diamond icing pattern across its top. The other cupcake was a bright orange-pinkish color and looked like it had a puff of cotton candy on top.

Xax stepped out of the bathroom with a shiny, clean face. "Private Blootin, have you decided which cupcake Private Splattly will eat?"

"I'm deciding," Auggie told him. "And stop acting like such a dope. I think all this power's gone straight to your head."

Xax put his hand on Auggie's shoulder and gave it a hard squeeze.

"Hey!" Auggie shouted, pushing his brother back. "What's the matter with you?"

"Don't challenge me, Private," Xax told his brother. "A general is always correct. Now which cupcake have you chosen?"

Auggie picked up the red one. "This one," he said, handing it to Horace.

"Good choice," Xax said. "Time to chow down, Private Splattly. Don't be afraid."

Horace chuckled. "Uh, General, it's hard not to be afraid. I don't know what it will do to me."

Xax stuck out his bottom lip. "Good point. Okay, Private, I give you permission to be a little afraid. Now go ahead and eat your cupcake like a man."

Horace put the pink cupcake in his backpack then picked up the red cupcake. When he looked at the icing closely, he could see that the center of each diamond had a tiny fountain on it spouting red goo. The goo was sticky and made his fingers tingle. Horace stuck the cupcake into his mouth and chewed.

Yuck! It may have looked like a cupcake, but it tasted and smelled like a mixture of onions, garlic, eggs, and mushrooms.

"Is it okay?" Auggie asked.

"How is the cupcake performing?" Xax asked.

Horace opened his mouth to answer, but instead of talking, red foam spilled from his mouth. He couldn't stop it. No matter how much he chewed and swallowed, the red froth kept coming. It dripped over his chin, down his chest, and onto his pants.

"Stop that!" Xax commanded. "That stuff is stinking up the whole hut."

"It's the cupcake that's doing it," Auggie told his brother. "Are you okay, Horace?"

Horace chewed and swallowed, finally getting the last of the cupcake down. The frothing stopped, and he took a deep breath. "Well, I'm glad that's done."

Auggie leaned in, sniffed, and looked at Horace's arm. "Uh, you reek of something gross. And red drippy stuff is coming out of your skin."

Horace lifted an arm. Red ooze was coming out of it, and his body tingled. "I think something's happening. I can't feel my arms and legs." He waved his arms and stomped his feet.

"I can move them, but I can't feel them." And then right before the boys' eyes, Horace's arms and legs shrank and shrank and shrank until all that was left of him was a torso with a head on top.

"What's happening?!" Xax shouted. "What did your sister put in that cupcake?!"

"This is crazy!" Auggie shouted.

"I can't stop it," Horace said. And just as he said that, his body began stretching. It became longer and longer. Sharp fangs stuck out of his mouth and dripped red ooze. His skin turned silvery and broke out in a pattern of bright red diamonds. Horace lay on the floor, rolling back and forth. "What happened?" he asked.

Xax and Auggie backed away from him.

Horace slid his body across the floor, stretched, and looked in the mirror above the bathroom sink. He had the head of a boy and the body of a diamondback rattlesnake!

"I'm a Splattlesnake," Horace said, grinning with his oozing fangs.

BLOOTINITE FOUND!

Y ou think this is funny?" Auggie asked.

Horace raised his body and stood on his rattling tail. He was as tall as the hut's ceiling! "Look at me!"

"You're a giant boy-snake!" Xax said.

Horace laughed. "It's because of the cupcake. It won't last for more than a few hours." He whipped his rattle through the air. "Doesn't that sound scary? I wonder what my venom does. It tastes like garlic, onions, and a little paprika."

Xax held out a hand. "I order you not to bite me, Private Splattly," he said.

Auggie nudged his brother with an elbow.

"Order him not to bite me, too," he said.

Horace lowered himself to the floor. "I'm not going to bite either of you. Now help me get into my Cupcaked Crusader costume so no one knows who I am. Without arms or legs, it might be hard to put it on."

Ten minutes later, Horace's costume was on. Sort of. The boys pulled the mask over Horace's head. The cape, arms, and legs dangled from where Horace's neck usually was.

"This is good," Horace said. "Now I just have to find my sister."

Auggie tossed up his hands. "How can you if you're so low to the ground?"

"Don't worry. I'll figure it out." He raised his rattle, saluting Xax. "Does Private Splattly have permission to go on his mission, General Blootin?" he asked.

Xax shook with fear at the site of Horace's dripping fangs. He began counting the red diamonds on Horace's body. "Eleven, twelve . . . Uh, yeah . . . Sure . . ."

Horace gave his tail a rattle, then slithered out of the hut.

• • •

Laffy Woods was dark even in the daytime. The thick branches and large leaves of the trees blocked sunlight from reaching the ground.

Hahahahaha.

Hushed laughter sounded through the trees. Horace slithered across the ground, hiding behind bushes, weeds, and rocks.

Hahahahaha.

He swiveled his head in every direction, trying to see what was making all that noise. Was that a Clownosaurus? Horace wasn't sure since he'd never seen one before. Were they small? Large? Fat or thin? What if they were *invisible?*

Horace coiled himself tight, making sure he didn't rattle his tail and attract attention. He waited.

Hahahahaha.

The laughing grew louder. A loud, thunderous pounding vibrated through the ground.

Trees swayed. Branches snapped and fell to the ground.

Boom. Boom. Boom. Boom.

Horace peeked out from behind a fallen tree in time to see two huge feet stomp down, smashing the ground right beside his body. Each of the giant feet was attached to a giant leg that was attached to a giant creature that rose fifty feet into the air. The bottom half of the monster was shaped like an elephant. The top half looked like a Tyrannosaurus rex. But this animal was different from anything Horace had ever seen before. It was as white as snow, with large colorful spots covering its body from head to toe. A wild bush of bright orange hair grew from its head, ankles, and wrists.

Hahahahaha, the Clownosaurus laughed in a loud, low voice. The monster clomped through the woods, breaking trees.

"Oh no! Run!"

"My Blootinite Detector is going crazy! We must be really close to finding it!"

"Melody, we've got to hide! A monster's coming!"

That was Betsy and Melody! Horace had to find them before the Clownosaurus did. He slithered over to a tall tree, wrapped his body around its trunk, and pulled himself higher and higher. The bark itched his skin. Twice Horace had to lean down and scratch himself with his teeth.

Horace made it to the top, clung tightly to a branch, and spied the huge Clownosaurus towering over the troop of girls from the Mangler hut.

"Eeeeek!"

Hahahahaha, the Clownosaurus laughed. "Do you think it's okay to come into my woods and take things away from me? I don't think so!"

Betsy backed against a tree. "We're just looking for Blootinite. We don't want to take anything from you."

"Hah!" the Clownosaurus roared. "You'll steal from me just the way the lady did."

"What lady?" Melody asked.

"Don't pretend you don't know what I'm

talking about," the Clownosaurus boomed. He leaned over, picked up Betsy with a claw, and breathed in her face. "Hello, little girl. I think it's time I stole all your laughs away."

Melody ran up to the monster and smashed the heel of her Lily Deaver hiking boot on its toe. "You put her down now!" She held up her Blootinite Detector and aimed it at the monster. "If you don't put Betsy down, I'll turn on my machine, and it will melt all your spots." Melody's earlobes wiggled, and Horace knew she was making it up. Her earlobes always wiggled when she lied.

Hahahahaha, the Clownosaurus laughed.

Melody threw a switch, and the orange light flashed really fast.

The Clownosaurus's spots didn't melt, but a strange blue glow came from its mouth. The Clownosaurus growled.

"Turn that off," Betsy screamed. "You're making it angry!"

Horace watched from the top of the tree. The

monster grabbed Melody in its hand and lifted her to its face. The Blootinite Detector flashed even brighter than before.

Hahahahaha, the monster laughed. He opened his mouth wide, showing his teeth. There were hundreds of them, and each one was a sparkly bright blue. They were exactly the same color as Auggie and Xax's lucky coins.

"Blootinite found! Blootinite found!" the Blootinite Detector sang. Melody's machine worked! She'd discovered it! The rarest stone ever wasn't really hidden deep inside Rumbly Mountain. Blootinite came from the teeth of a Clownosaurus—teeth that were about to chomp down on Melody!

Horace had to save his sister. He uncoiled himself from the tree and flung his snake body into the air. The Cupcaked Crusader had sprung into action!

SNAKEBITE

Thwack!

Horace landed right on top of the Clownosaurus's head in his patch of bright orange hair. "Put them down now!" he commanded.

The Clownosaurus waved the claws that held Melody and Betsy. "You better not be messing up my hair!" he roared. "It took me two hours to fluff it this morning!"

Horace smashed his rattle between the Clownosaurus's eyes.

"Youch!" the monster screamed.

Horace slid down the monster's arm and wrapped his snake body around Betsy, pulling her from the monster's grip. Betsy beat her fists against Horace's body. "You put me down!" she screamed.

"Youch! I'm the Cupcaked Crusader. I'm here to save you!" Horace told her.

Betsy kept pounding her fists. "Well, you don't have to be so gross and scary!" she yelled. "Why'd you have to be a snake?"

Horace wanted to tell Betsy that she should ask his sister, but he kept his mouth shut.

Melody hollered at Horace from the monster's other claw. "Can't you ever save me first?" she asked.

Horace set Betsy on the ground. The Clownosaurus roared with anger and lifted Melody to his mouth. Horace didn't have enough time to slither up and grab his sister from the monster's claw. There was only one thing he could do.

Horace opened his mouth and sank his fangs

into the Clownosaurus's big toe. Horace felt the venom drip from his fangs into the monster.

"Yarggghhhhh!" the monster moaned. He opened his claw, grabbed his toe, and let Melody drop through the air.

Horace swung his tail into the air, caught his sister, and stood her on the ground.

The Clownosaurus bared his large Blootinite teeth. Horace saw that two of them were missing. The Clownosaurus reached out with a claw to take a swipe at Horace, then suddenly

stopped midswing. The monster got a very scared look on his face and began crying. Large tears dripped from his eyes, and he frowned. "Why did you have to be so mean?" he yelled. "I'm going to go tell my mommy on you!" The Clownosaurus ran off into the woods.

Horace's venom had made the monster into a crybaby!

Horace slithered over to the Mangler girls. "Is everyone okay?" he asked. "You shouldn't be out in the woods when such dangerous creatures are loose." He stared at his sister. "Don't you think you should go back to camp, young lady?"

Melody stood before her brother. "I think the Cupcaked Crusader should mind his own business," she said.

Betsy gave Horace a pat on the back. "Be nice to the Cupcaked Crusader. He saved our lives," she scolded.

Melody switched on her Blootinite Detector. The light didn't flash. "He also scared away the

source of the Blootinite," she said. "Now we'll have to find the Clownosaurus again."

Horace thought maybe he should bite Melody, so she'd become a crybaby, too, and run back to camp. He smiled, but knew that if he did bite his sister, she'd probably be mad at him for-ever. He flicked his tail at her, lightly touching the tip of her nose. "I advise you to stay away from that monster. The crybaby venom won't last very long, and then it will be angry again. Why would you want to put yourself in danger just to get one of his teeth? That's crazy."

Melody put her hands on her hips. "Look, Cupcaked Crusader, you did your job and saved us. Now go away. We have work to do." She turned to the other girls. "Okay, Manglers, let's set up camp. Later tonight, we'll find the Clownosaurus while it's asleep and take out its teeth. I have some painkiller I made with my Lily Deaver Spill & Brew Laboratory, so the monster won't feel a thing." She grinned at Horace. "Not only will I be richer than Penny Honey, but I'll also be famous for discovering a new creature. How about that, Cupcaked Crusader?"

Horace bit his lip to stop from yelling at his sister. The only reason she was doing this was so she could be richer than Penny Honey. *He* had to save his sister, the teachers, *and* catch a Clownosaurus so he'd become famous and no one would ever make fun of him for being little.

"Leave the monster alone," he told her. "Let a superhero like me take care of him."

Melody leaned close to her brother's ear. "I only gave you that snake cupcake in case I needed you to slither inside holes to help me find the Blootinite. But now that I know where it is, I don't need you anymore." She turned her back on her brother and smiled at the other girls. "You know what? I bet if we found some of the monster's baby teeth, we could make matching Blootinite rings. Penny Honey will be mad with jealousy!"

The girls jumped up and down with excitement. None of them even cared about the Cupcaked Crusader anymore. Melody glanced over her shoulder and gave her brother a wink. "Bye-bye, superhero. Thanks for your help." Then she walked away and began setting up her tent.

Chapter 13

THE SCARE OF THE CLOWNOSAURUS, PARTS 1 & 2

While Horace was slithering out of the forest, his arms and legs grew back, and his fangs shrank back into normal boy teeth. He stood and bent his knees and elbows.

"Yep, everything's working the way it's supposed to," he said. He wiggled his fingers in his face. "I missed having you guys. I wonder if snakes miss having fingers. But I guess that since they *never* had fingers, they can't really *miss* having them."

After doing a quick stretch, Horace ran back to the Inchworm hut and changed from his

Cupcaked Crusader costume into jeans and a shirt. Then he packed his knapsack and raced to the Cougar hut to meet up with Auggie and Xax.

"There's no way we can let Melody find the Clownosaurus first," he told the twins. "And your lucky coins are made from the teeth of a Clownosaurus! That's where your great-great-, not-so-great, pretty good grandmother must have got Blootinite."

Auggie and Xax sat on their beds that looked like the benches that kids sat on outside Principal's Nosair office at school. The whole hut looked like the principal's office. The sink was inside a filing cabinet, and a bulletin board on the wall had a list of names of kids who had to stay after school.

Auggie pulled the chain from under his shirt and held up the shiny blue coin. "This is Blootinite?" he asked.

"That one little coin is probably worth tons of money," Horace said. "It's what Melody's trying to get in the forest."

Xax put a hand to his chest, holding the coin that he kept on the chain under his sweater. "I wonder if our dad knew how valuable this was when he gave it to us? I bet he didn't." He began rearranging his thirty-one pairs of identical white socks. "Maybe we shouldn't go after the Clownosaurus. It sounds dangerous."

"But you're General Xax, the leader," Horace said. "If my sister's not afraid, why should you be?"

Xax stacked his socks in a pyramid. "Sometimes a leader has to decide what not to do. That's the kind of leader I am."

Auggie put his Blootinite coin in his eye like a monocle. "I would like to see a Clownosaurus," he said. "Don't you wonder how our great-great-, not-so-great, pretty good grandmother got these from the Clownosaurus?"

"Of course," Xax answered. "I just don't want to get eaten while finding out."

Horace put on his backpack and went to the hut door.

Auggie got off his bed and joined him. "Well, if you're too afraid to go, I guess I'll have to lead us," he said.

"But I'm General Xax, the great leader," Xax said, grabbing his empty knapsack.

"Then come on," Auggie said. "Get leading."

Xax spun in a circle, not sure what to pack and what not to pack. Finally, he just raked his arm across the top of his dresser, pushing all thirty-one pairs of socks into his backpack. "All right, Private Blootin and Private Splattly, hup-hup-hup!" he shouted, and rushed out the door.

• • •

Horace and the twins hiked through Laffy Woods, stopping at the spot where Horace had last seen the Mangler girls. The sun was setting behind Rumbly Mountain, and the air grew thick with fog.

Xax sat on a log. "I thought you said they were setting up camp here," he said. "How can I lead if you're giving me the wrong information?" He kicked off his hiking boots and stretched his toes.

Auggie sat next to his brother and unlaced his boots. "I bet they were already eaten by the Clownosaurus," he said.

"D-don't say that," Xax said nervously.

"The Clownosaurus doesn't eat people. It only makes it so people can't laugh anymore," Horace said.

"Are you sure?" Auggie asked.

Horace didn't answer. The truth was, he didn't know for sure if the Clownosaurus ate people or not. That big Clownosaurus had sure looked like it was going to eat his sister. He took out the magnifying glass that was attached to his canteen. He held it over something he spotted on the ground, took a pair of tweezers from his backpack, and picked up a bright orange hair. "This must have come from the Clownosaurus," he said. He crawled across the ground and picked up a strand of purple yarn. "And this must have fallen off Melody's sweater I made last week."

"We already knew the Clownosaurus was here before," Auggie said.

"Your evidence is not very helpful, Private Splattly," Xax said, rubbing his toes. "And I need a foot massage. Which one of you is going to rub my important General Xax toes?"

There was a rustling in the bushes. Horace and the twins turned around. Through the dim light, the boys saw a flash of white leg with a

large blue spot. The three ten-year-olds stopped talking and jumped behind the log, pressing their bellies as close to the ground as possible.

"It's the Clownosaurus!" Horace whispered.

"He ate the Manglers for dinner and now he's going to eat us for dessert," Auggie said.

The boys shook with fear. They could hear the sound of leaves crunching under the Clownosaurus's feet.

And then it appeared. A small dark figure walked closer to the log.

"It must be a baby Clownosaurus," Horace whispered.

"Eat your other cupcake!" Xax squealed. "That's an order!"

The baby Clownosaurus stood on the log right in front of the boys. Suddenly a flashlight shined down on them.

"No fair! Don't hide!"

The boys looked up. Standing on the log above them was Petie Bloog in his clown suit.

"Petie, what are you doing here?" Horace asked. He stood and brushed off his clothes.

"This is no place for a little kid," Auggie said, standing.

Xax remained crouching behind the log. "How do we know you're not a Clownosaurus disguised as a little boy?" he asked.

Petie frowned, and his eyes began to water. "I'm a boy! I'm five!" he cried, holding up a hand and spreading his fingers. "I escaped from the hut and ran here so Cyrus couldn't get me."

Xax stood. "Privates, let's huddle and discuss."

The three older boys formed a circle.

Xax started talking fast. "Okay, soldiers, I've heard that sometimes enemies like to wear disguises so they look like they're on our side. Maybe this kid is really a Clownosaurus."

Horace bit his lip to keep from laughing. "Uh, Xax, he really is Petie. The Clownosaurus was much, much bigger."

"Come on, Xax. Petie can't walk back to camp alone now that it's dark," Auggie said.

"Well, then I guess we have to let him stay, huh?" Xax said.

"True," Horace said. "And we can't let Cyrus hurt him."

They opened their circle and looked at Petie.

"All right, Private Bloog," Xax said. "Welcome to Team Xax."

• • •

The boys lay in their sleeping bags, zipped tightly inside their tent. Each held a flashlight under his chin, shining at his face.

Clomp-clomp-clomp! Hahahahahahaha!

"What's that?" Xax asked.

"That's the Clownosaurus!" Auggie said.

"I wanna go back," Petie said. "I wanna be in jail, far away from Clownosaurus."

"So do I," Auggie said.

"I totally agree," Xax said.

The footsteps and laughing grew louder. *Clomp-clomp-clomp!! Hahahahahahaha!!*

Horace sat up. "But we can't go back now. My sister's out there somewhere. She could be in danger," he said.

"What about us? We're in danger now!" Xax shouted.

"Don't you hear the Clownosaurus?" Auggie asked.

They turned their heads, shining their spot-lights at the tent's sides.

Clomp-clomp! Haha! The stomping and laughing grew louder. *Clomp-clomp! Haha!* The noise seemed to be coming from all around them.

"How can it be everywhere at once?" Xax asked.

And then the boys heard the loudest laugh they had every heard in their lives. It sounded as loud as a thousand mean clowns laughing at one thousand mean jokes.

Hahahahahaha! Hahahahahaha! Hahaha-hahaha!

Four giant Clownosaurus claws tore open the tent, and four giant Clownosauruses stood laughing at the boys. But unlike the first Clownosaurus Horace met, which had different-colored spots, the spots on these Clowno-sauruses were all yellow. Their blue Blootinite teeth glowed in the dark, lighting up the night sky.

AAAAAAAAAEEEEEEEEEEEEEEEEEEE AAAAAAAAAAAAAEEEEEEEEEEEEEEEEE EKKKKKKKKKKKKKKKKKKK! Auggie, Xax, Petie, and Horace screamed as loud as one thou-sand scared boys screaming at one thousand scary monsters.

One Clownosaurus grabbed Auggie in a claw and ran off into the woods.

One Clownosaurus grabbed Xax in a claw and ran off into the woods.

Horace reached into his backpack with both hands. There had to be something in there that could help. He pulled out the first things his hands touched.

Two giant rolls of Sweet Cheeks Toilet Tissue!

Horace couldn't have been happier that his mom had made him bring it with him to camp. He tossed a roll to Petie. "T-P the Clownosauruses!" he yelled. "Watch me!" Horace tossed the roll of toilet paper at a Clownosaurus. It wrapped all around the monster's head and dropped to the ground. Horace picked it up again and threw it as hard as he could. The toilet paper tangled all around the monster's arms and legs. "Help! Help! Help!" the Clownosaurus yelped, spinning in circles and running off into the woods.

"Get the other one!" Horace told Petie.

Petie hurled his roll of toilet paper at the other Clownosaurus. It got stuck on one of the monster's teeth. When the Clownosaurus tried to shake it off, the toilet paper wrapped all around its face, so it couldn't see where it was going. "Help! Help! Help!" the Clownosaurus cried, bumping into trees and running off into the woods.

Horace and Petie fell to the ground, out of breath.

"I have a feeling that trying to catch a Clownosaurus for a pet isn't such a good idea," Horace said.

THE LAST LAUGH?

The boys sat in the ruins of their camp. The Clownosauruses had destroyed the tent and crushed a lot of their supplies. Horace's canteen had been poked with a claw, and all the water had dripped out. The compass was bent in half. The sleeping bags had been torn to shreds, and all the stuffing had come out and was floating around the boys' heads.

"Wish Cupcaked Crusader was here," Petie said. "He help us."

Horace picked up his backpack and looked inside. His second cupcake was still there, but it was kind of smooshed. "Maybe the Cupcaked Crusader could help, but maybe not," he said.

"He saves everyone!" Petie said. "Cupcaked Crusader is great!"

Horace gave Petie a pat on the back. "I bet you're right," he said. "And maybe he'll come by real soon."

"He will," Petie said.

Horace switched on his flashlight and pointed it at the ground. The first thing he had to do was find out where the Clownosauruses lived. He spotted a trail of footprints in the dirt. They led through the woods in the direction of Rumbly Mountain. "Okay, Petie, let's start hiking. Keep your flashlight on the ground and your eyes on the tracks. We're going to save everyone tonight."

Petie gasped. "I don't wanna! I don't know how!"

Horace looked at him. "Well, you're going to have to learn how," he told Petie. "If you don't, a lot of kids and teachers could be in big trouble.

The Clownosauruses could make it so they never laugh again. Do you want that to happen?"

Petie shook his head. "No," he said.

"Then let's get tracking. I have a feeling the Cupcaked Crusader will be around real soon to help us," Horace told him.

The two boys aimed their flashlights at the ground, keeping their eyes fixed on the huge Clownosaurus footprints on the forest floor. They took step after step, walking deeper and deeper into the foggy darkness of Laffy Woods.

Hahahahahahaha . . .

The two boys walked farther up the mountain. The laughing got louder.

"W-we're getting close," Horace said, his voice trembling with fear. "Are you afraid?" he asked Petie.

Petie picked his nose, lifted his shirt, and stuck his finger in his belly button. "I dunno," he said. "Is Cupcaked Crusader here soon?"

Horace didn't answer. He didn't want to tell Petie that even he didn't know how the Cupcaked Crusader would be able to save everyone from *four* Clownosauruses.

Straight ahead of the two boys stood **Rumbly Mountain**. It looked as though it was over ten thousand feet high with a huge cave at the bottom. Bright blue light spilled out of the cave.

"Get down," Horace warned. He took Petie by the arm and pulled him behind a rock. Horace lifted his head and looked into the mouth of the cave.

There weren't four Clownosauruses.

Horace counted one-two-three-four-five-six of them!

Six Clownosauruses were running around the inside of the cave doing weird tricks! One Clownosaurus stuck a bird up his nose and sang songs while the bird flapped its wings against his face. The second and third Clownosauruses put huge mushrooms on their heads and danced like ballerinas. The fourth Clownosaurus painted faces on her yellow spots and pretended they were talking to one another. And the fifth

Clownosaurus stuck his head in a tree stump and did back flips.

The last Clownosaurus was the biggest one of all and the only one with different-colored spots. He was the monster that Horace had seen that afternoon with Melody. He held a large white feather in his claw and was pointing it at a group of people.

Auggie, Xax, Melody, and the four other Manglers, Professor Nosair, Mr. Dienow, Sir Stickle, and the other teachers were tied to rocks and watching like an audience. All of them were dressed in clown suits just like Petie's, and all of them had red noses on their faces that blinked on and off. They were laughing so hard that their mouths hung wide open and drool dripped down their chins. The biggest Clownosaurus took his feather and stuck it in Mr. Dienow's nose, making him scream with laughter.

Horace couldn't believe it! Mr. Dienow was so mean, but now he was laughing! Horace

didn't think his science teacher knew how to laugh.

The big Clownosaurus took his feather out of Dienow's nose and tickled Xax's ear. Xax began laughing so hard that his eyes looked like they were going to pop out of his head.

"What are the monsters doing?" Petie asked.

Horace raked his hand through his short, spiky hair. "They're making everyone use up all their laughs so they can never laugh again," he said. "Then they'll be sad for the rest of their lives." He reached into his backpack, grabbed his Cupcaked Crusader costume, and the pink cupcake his sister gave him. He hid the costume and cupcake under his sweatshirt. "Okay, Petie. You stay here and don't move an inch. I have to get a closer look at what's happening in the cave."

Petie grabbed Horace's arm. "No!" he screamed. "Don't!"

Horace shook Petie off. "Quiet down or the Clownosauruses will find us. If you want to help, be on the lookout for more of them."

Petie stuck a finger in his nose and then stuck it in his belly button.

Horace kept himself from laughing and gave Petie a salute. "All right, Private Bloog. Good luck on your mission."

Petie smiled. "I'll be a good soldier," he said.

Horace nodded. "I'm sure you will."

Horace got down on his hands and knees, crawling through the woods to make sure none of the Clownosauruses spotted him. Once he got far enough away from Petie, he put on his costume and took another look at the cave.

Now three of the Clownosauruses were playing a game of leapfrog. They hopped over one another, fell on their heads, and rolled in the dirt. Two others played kickball, but instead of using a ball, they used a watermelon. One Clownosaurus kicked it and splattered seeds and mush all over the other Clownosaurus.

Sir Stickle, the teachers, and all the kids were laughing so hard that it looked as if their wide-open mouths had swallowed the rest of their heads.

Horace held the pink cupcake in his open palm. The puffy pink cotton-candy top had been smooshed, and the side was dented. But it still looked pretty good to Horace.

What powers had his sister put into this pink cupcake? Were they *real* superpowers or just something dumb like knitting-needle hands or dustpan feet for floor cleaning?

Horace didn't know. He only knew he had to do something to save everyone before every single one of their laughs was gone.

So without another thought, Horace stuck the pink cupcake in his mouth and chewed.

A Bucketful of Horace

It was the most delicious cupcake Horace had ever tasted! It was sweet and gooey, with peppermint cotton-candy icing on the top and cherry cream in the middle. The cake was as light and fluffy as a cloud.

It was the most perfect cupcake ever!

Horace finished eating the cupcake. The weird thing about it was that even though it was pretty small, it felt like it filled up his stomach, as if he'd eaten twenty cupcakes.

His stomach began to ache. It felt as if something was inside it and trying to push its way out. Horace poked his belly with a finger. His stomach felt hard, like it was made out of metal.

Then it began growing.

And growing.

And growing.

His stomach pushed out and became a huge bucket hanging off the front of his body! A second later, one of his hands turned into a pick to break rocks, and the other became a sledgehammer. Both were so heavy, Horace had to hunch over and drag them across the ground to keep from falling over.

Horace knew why his sister had given him these cupcakes—she had thought Blootinite was buried inside Rumbly Mountain and wanted Horace to have powers that would help her get it out.

But Blootinite wasn't in Rumbly Mountain. It was inside the mouths of the Clownosauruses.

So now the Cupcaked Crusader had to figure out a way to use the powers to save everyone from the Clownosauruses.

Horace looked at the cave and watched

as the Clownosauruses started playing Duck-Duck-Goose. The kids and teachers laughed even louder. Their red noses were blinking so fast they looked like a line of Christmas lights.

Except for Sir Stickle and Ms. Wobbley-knees. He had completely stopped laughing, and she was chuckling very quietly.

Horace slowly walked forward, dragging his sledgehammer and pick hands across the ground and into the cave. "Hey, everyone," he yelled. "The Cupcaked Crusader is here to save you!"

The Clownosauruses stopped playing their game and looked at him. The kids and teachers all stopped laughing and looked at the super-hero with the big bucket stomach.

Loud sounds of laughter filled the air.

But it wasn't coming from the kids and teachers . . .

It was coming from the Clownosauruses! The monsters were rolling on the ground, laughing as hard as they could.

"Look!" One Clownosaurus laughed. "Bucket Man is here!"

"That's the puniest superhero I ever saw!" another Clownosaurus guffawed.

Five of the Clownosauruses clutched their stomachs, bursting with laughter. All except for the biggest, who stood leaning against the side of the cave, gritting his sharp blue teeth.

Horace tried to lift an arm and hit it against the wall to scare the laughing Clownosauruses.

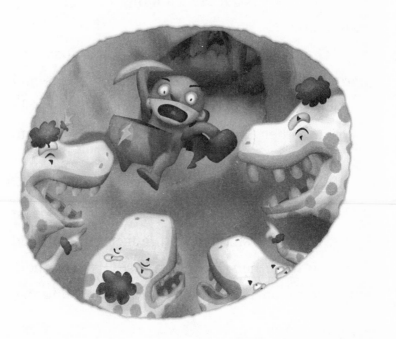

He swung his arm up, then lost his balance and fell on his back with his bucket belly sticking up in the air. His arms were so heavy he couldn't even sit. "Hey!" he yelled at the Clownosauruses. "You're not supposed to laugh at a superhero. That's very impolite."

The Clownosauruses laughed even louder. In fact, they were laughing so hard that all their bright yellow spots grew smiley faces. "Make him stop! Make him stop!" one yelled.

"No more! No more!" another cried, holding his sides.

"*Grrrrrrrrrrrrr,*" the largest Clownosaurus growled. He was so mad that all his spots had turned a fiery, hot red. "That's enough!" he told all the other Clownosauruses. "Don't let him control you! People are the enemy!"

The other Clownosauruses kept laughing. They couldn't stop. The spots on the biggest Clownosaurus smoked with anger. He stomped over to the other Clownosauruses, picked them up one by one, and tossed them into the forest.

"Don't come back until you stop laughing!" he yelled.

"Hooray for the Cupcaked Crusader," Sir Stickle cheered. "You're here just in time. I think I used up all my giggles and most of my snickers."

Ms. Wobbleyknees nodded her head. "I used up all my chuckles, but I still have lots of guffaws, chortles, howls, hoots, whinnies, snorts, and cackles."

Xax wrinkled his brow. "I used up all my yucks, but still have lots of other kinds of laughs."

Melody rolled her eyes. "Hurry up and untie us, Cupcaked Crusader."

Horace lay on the ground. "I think my powers don't let me untie anything," he said, trying to lift his arms, but failing. "Too bad I don't have powers that will let me untie you, little girl," he said, glaring at his sister. "I guess all my powers are good for is getting Blootinite."

"Oh, so you're here to get Blootinite, too?"

the largest Clownosaurus growled, stomping back into the cave. "Then it's too bad you didn't get away while you had the chance." He picked Horace up with one claw. "I don't usually like to eat superheroes just before bed, but I think I will tonight." He took Horace's pick hand and slammed it into the side of the cave. The Cupcaked Crusader hung from the wall like a Christmas ornament from a tree.

The Clownosaurus laughed a mean laugh at the superhero. "And now I think it's time I practiced some of my spitting tricks on my enemy."

To Tell the Teeth

The monster puckered his lips and spit a giant wad of spit right at Horace.

Clang.

Horace looked down. The huge blob of spit had landed right inside his bucket belly.

"Hahahahaha! Bull's-eye!" the Clownosaurus roared. He sucked in and spit again.

Splot!

Another glob of spit landed in the bucket belly. It was almost full to the top.

Splish! Splam!

Spit sloshed over the rim of the bucket.

Splosh! Sploosh!

The Clownosaurus kept spitting into the bucket. Waves crashed over its brim and burst in Horace's face. It was like he had been tied to the mast of a large ship in the middle of a hurricane. Rolling waves of spit kept splashing in his face. If it didn't stop soon, he was afraid he might drown.

From down below, Horace could hear the cries of his friends and teachers.

"Hang in there, Cupcaked Crusader!" Xax called.

"You can do it!" Auggie said.

"Get down here and save us right now!" Dienow yelled.

The Clownosaurus roared with laughter. He rolled a big ball of spit on his tongue and prepared to fire it at the half-pint-size superhero.

Horace knew he had to save himself. It was now or never. With all the strength he had in his body, he lifted his sledgehammer arm and slammed it into his bucket belly. All the spit flew out like a tidal wave, crashing onto the floor of the cave where the Clownosaurus stood.

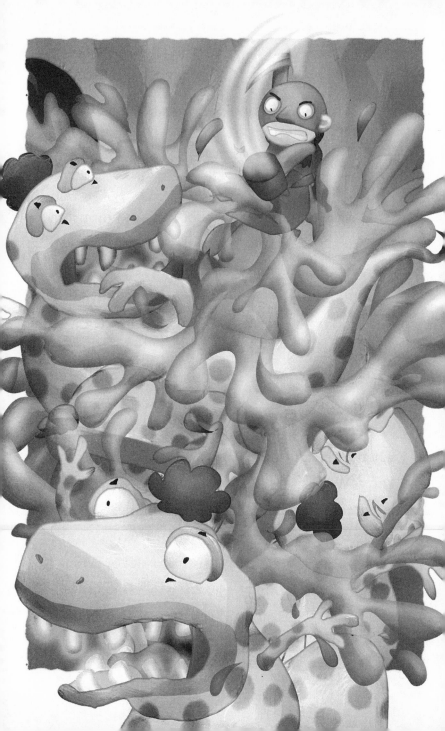

"Whoa!" the Clownosaurus yelled. He slipped in the spit and fell to the ground. The Clownosaurus immediately grabbed his foot and held it in his claws. "Ouchie-ouch-ouch! You made me twist my ankle," he yelled. "Why'd you have to do that, meanie!"

Horace pointed his foot at the monster. "You're the meanie! You were trying to drown me in your spit and tied up all these people and were taking their laughs away. You even tried to eat Melody in the woods. Why do you want to do that?"

The Clownosaurus rubbed his ankle and opened his mouth, showing the two holes where his teeth were missing. "A long, long time ago, when I was a little Clownosaurus, a lady came to Laffy Woods. I had toothaches in two of my teeth, and I asked if she could help me. She told me to go to sleep and that when I woke up the pain would be gone. So I went to sleep. When I woke up, my toothaches were gone, but so were my teeth! Ever since, I've always known that people were mean and that whenever they come into Laffy Woods, I know they're going to try and steal my teeth." A large tear rolled out of the Clownosaurus's eye. "It's not easy to eat without teeth, you know."

Horace shook his head. "You know, maybe that lady didn't think you wanted your teeth anymore. Maybe it was a mistake," he said. He looked over at his sister. "And *most* people are nice and would never try to take your teeth even if they were worth a gazillion dollars. And to prove it, I know where you can get back the teeth you lost."

The Clownosaurus stared up at him. "My teeth?!" he cried. "Did you help that lady take them!?"

"No no no," Horace said. "But I do know where they are. I'll give them back if you promise to let us go and never take anyone's laughs again." He pointed his feet at Auggie and Xax. "Just get me down and untie those two boys, and you'll have your teeth back."

The Clownosaurus reached up a claw, pulled Horace from the wall, and set him on the ground. Then he untied Auggie and Xax.

"Boys, I think you each have something around your necks that belongs to this Clownosaurus," Horace said in his Cupcaked Crusader voice.

Auggie scrunched his mouth up. "But our great-great-, not-so-great, pretty good grandmother Serena Blootin got these," he said. "They belong to our family."

"They belong to the Clownosaurus," Horace said.

Xax turned to Auggie. "As leader of this mission, I order you to turn your lucky Blootinite coin over to the Cupcaked Crusader," he ordered. "It was good that Serena helped the Clownosaurus get rid of his toothaches, but she should never have taken his teeth."

Xax took the Blootinite coin from around his neck and removed it from the chain. Auggie did the same.

"My teeth!" the Clownosaurus yelled happily, taking them from Auggie and Xax.

Melody spun to face Auggie. "You've had Blootinite all these years and never did anything with it?!" she shouted. "That must be why my Blootinite Detector went off in the bus."

"Just put them back in your mouth where they belong," Horace said.

The Clownosaurus set the coins in his mouth. The two holes were filled, but both teeth were still loose. "They won't stay," he said.

"Hmmmm," Horace thought. He tried to get into his thinking pose, but his arms were too heavy to lift to his head. Finally he thought of something. "Hey," he called. "Lift me into your mouth."

The Clownosaurus picked Horace up and held him inside his mouth. Horace lifted his sledgehammer hand and very gently rapped it against each tooth, knocking them back into place so they wouldn't wobble.

The Clownosaurus set Horace on the ground

and smiled a perfect Blootinite smile. "Thanks!" he said. "I guess most people *are* nice."

Xax stepped forward. "As General Blootin, I want to apologize for Serena Blootin. I'm sure she didn't know you'd want your teeth after she took them out."

The Clownosaurus accepted the apology and untied everyone. All the teachers and kids in their clown suits stretched their arms and legs.

Principal Nosair shook the Cupcaked

Crusader's pick hand. "Thank you for your help. I'll make sure we put up a plaque in the school with your name on it," he said.

"Thanks, Principal Nosair," Horace said. He leaned over to Melody and whispered in her ear, "Next time give me powers that help better. I almost couldn't save us with these ones."

Melody folded her arms across her chest. "A genius like me doesn't have to explain herself to less-smart people like you," she said. "And next time I want to get rich, I'll make sure I discover a priceless gem that comes from the ground, and *not* from the mouth of a monster." She sniffed the air and wrinkled her nose. "Yeck!" she moaned, turning to Betsy and the other Manglers. "The Cupcaked Crusader smells like Clownosaurus spit!"

The girls laughed.

Horace sniffed his arm and laughed. "You're right!" he said. "I do." He walked up to Mr. Dienow. "Aren't you going to thank me for saving you?" he asked.

The science teacher pulled at his blinking red nose, but it wouldn't come loose. He scowled at the Cupcaked Crusader. "I'll never thank you for anything," he said. As he turned to storm out of the cave, they heard a loud rumble.

Carrumph-Carrumph-Carrumph!

Dienow jumped behind the Cupcaked Crusader and covered his head with his hands. "Save me!" he screamed. "The sky is falling! The sky is falling!"

The rumbling grew louder. Suddenly Petie Bloog rode into the cave on the backs of the five other Clownosauruses, who were piled in a pyramid. "Hey! Look at my new friends!" Petie yelled.

Horace looked at the science teacher crouching in fear behind him. "Ha!" he said, and everyone laughed, even the Clownosauruses.

Chapter 17

THE BEST BUNK-ALONG EVER

Hahahahahaha.

Laughter could be heard coming from every corner of the camp. It was the laughter of six Clownosauruses and a whole lot of kids having a great time at the Blootinville Elementary School Teacher Bunk-Along. The Clownosauruses splashed in the lake, wrestled on the lawn, and hung from the trees while kids climbed on their backs, bounced on their stomachs, and swung from their arms and legs. Some kids even sat on top of the Clownosauruses' heads and mussed their orange hair.

The Clownosauruses didn't even care that their hair was messed up. They were having a great time with their new friends.

Horace, Auggie, Xax, and Petie Bloog lay on the biggest Clownosaurus's stomach as he backpaddled around the lake.

"Ah, this is the life," Xax said, sipping a celernip soda. "I guess you all have to say I'm a great leader, huh?"

Auggie hung off the Clownosaurus's arm and kicked his legs in the water. "You're just lucky the Cupcaked Crusader came along," he told his twin. "And that Petie became friends with the other Clownosauruses."

Xax tapped a finger to his head. "That was all part of my plan," he said. "A good leader figures all that stuff out."

The Clownosaurus let out a loud chortle. "I never knew you people could be so much fun," he said. "I guess we didn't have to try and scare you away, after all."

Petie gave Horace a poke on the shoulder.

"See, Horace, you didn't have to be afraid and run back to camp last night. The Clowno-sauruses were really nice once we made friends and Melody put away her Blootinite Detector."

Horace rolled his eyes. Last night, after every-one was saved, he had to hurry back to camp as the Cupcaked Crusader before he changed back to his normal body. Then when everyone returned to camp, Horace pretended he'd got-ten scared and run back to the Inchworm hut instead of helping to save everyone. Now all the kids thought he was a big baby and that Petie was the coolest kid because he had made friends with the Clownosauruses.

Melody and Betsy were using their Lily Deaver scuba equipment to dive deep under Lake Honkaninny. Last night she'd told the Clownosauruses she was sorry for planning on taking their teeth. Because she couldn't have Blootinite, she came up with a new plan to get richer than Penny Honey. The two girls were searching for sunken treasure.

"There have to be some jewels here some-where, don't you think?" Melody asked Betsy.

Betsy nodded. "Hey, look over there!" she yelled.

All heads turned and looked across the lake. Penny Honey was skimming over the water on a solid-gold-and-diamond jet ski. "Hiya doodles, kids!" she sang. She rode so close to Melody and Betsy that she made a big wave crash over the girls' heads.

"That girl thinks she's so great!" Melody grumbled. "I want to buy a gold boat that can make an even bigger splash on Penny Honey!" The two girls dove under the water, searching for jewels.

"I guess this has been a pretty good week-end," Horace said, smiling at his friends.

Xax nodded. "Yep, and the best part is that Cyrus doesn't rule the camp anymore," he said.

"And that Sara doesn't have to be his girl-friend," Horace said.

The four boys looked to the shore. The big

wagon all the kids had built for Cyrus was finished and stood in the middle of the field. But instead of kids pulling Cyrus, Cyrus was pulling a Clownosaurus and Sara Willow. "Faster! Faster!" The Clownosaurus laughed. "Get a move on!"

Sara Willow's hair was shaped like the head of a Clownosaurus. She sat in the Clownosaurus's lap and poked Cyrus with a stick. "Why can't you go faster, little boy?"

Sweat dripped down Cyrus's face. He wrinkled his nose. "This is the worst Teacher Bunk-Along *ever*," he moaned.

All the teachers were floating on the lake in boats that had blackboard sails. While the kids tried to play, the teachers tried to teach them math, history, spelling, and Blootinographicalology.

There was only one subject missing a boat—science. Mr. Dienow was so upset that he'd had to be saved by the Cupcaked Crusader that he walked back to Blootinville the night before without even saying good-bye to his bunk of Inchworms.

Sir Stickle stood on the lifeguard tower with a giant bottle of rainbow glue. "Hear ye, hear ye!" he called. "I have a proclamation to make! In honor of our giant, spotted friends from Laffy Woods, I am pleased to announce that the name of Camp Blite will be changed to—"

Sir Stickle sprayed the glue high up in the air and spelled out C-A-M-P C-L-O-W-N-O-S-A-U-R-U-S. The letters hung in the air for a second, and all the kids, teachers, and Clownosauruses cheered.

Then the glue landed with a splat on Myrna Breckstein's head. Glue ran down her face in rainbow colors, and pine needles blew off the trees and stuck to her face.

"EEEE—YUCK!!" she cried.

Auggie, Xax, Horace, and the Clownosaurus all let out giant laughs as they splashed across Lake Honkaninny.

"I wish that friendly Cupcaked Crusader was

around to enjoy this fun day," the Clownosaurus said. "He's a great guy!"

Horace leaned across the Clownosaurus's belly and smiled. "I'll make sure I tell him next time he comes around," he said with a smile.

Lawrence David is 103 years old. He was a superhero for many years and had the power to eat lots and lots of candy bars without ever getting sick. Now he writes books and lives in New York City with his seven pet porcupines, named Radish, Macaroni, Wally, Simon, Sunshine, Persephone, and Dandelion.

Barry Gott is younger, but not by much. Although he has spent much of his life trying to bake superpower-giving cupcakes, the only superpower he's gotten is the ability to play the tuba and yodel at the same time. He has illustrated two other books about Horace as well as several picture books. He lives with his family, but no porcupines, in Ohio.

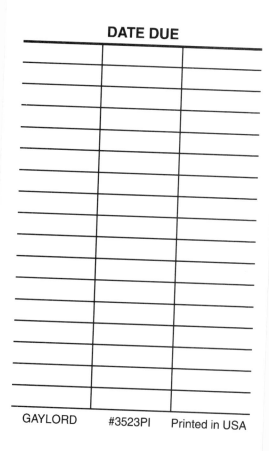

DATE DUE

GAYLORD   #3523PI   Printed in USA